This dragon book belongs to:

....

Teach Your Dragon To Understand Consequences
My Dragon Books - Volume 14
Written by Steve Herman

ISBN: 978-1948040389 (paperback)
ISBN: 978-1948040402 (hardcover)

www.MyDragonBooks.com

First Edition: July 2018

10 9 8 7 6 5 4 3 2 1

Hi! My name's Drew,
and I have something you've not seen...
It's a dragon of my own!
But don't worry; he's not mean.

I call him Diggory Doo;
he's a very special pet;
In fact, I bet he's just about
the best pet you can get!

A dragon must learn manners
and how to be polite,
So I had to teach my dragon
how to always do what's right.

Diggory ate some candy once,
but then when he was through,
He dropped the wrapper on the ground –
a bad thing to do!

Diggory loves the swings and slides
but hates to wait his turn;
He used to try to cut in line -
I told him he must learn...

That he should hold his horses
'til the other kids are done.
"It's no big deal," said Diggory Doo,
"I'm just having fun!"

Diggory stole some bubble gum
when he was at the store.
I told him, "That is so bad!
Don't do that anymore!"

He said, "I only took one piece;
I'm sure nobody saw.
I don't know why you're so upset
when I broke one little law."

Diggory skipped his homework once;
he didn't want to do it.
"Diggory Doo," I told him,
"this time I think you really blew it."

"For goodness sake!" said Diggory Doo.
"What difference does it make?
I just skipped homework once,
so I could take a little break."

"Diggory Doo," I asked my dragon, "have you not ever heard... That choices come with *consequences*? - You need to learn this word."

"Consequences" are results
of choices that we make;

Sometimes they help us see when we have made a big mistake.

If no one cleans their messes,
what a big mess that would be!

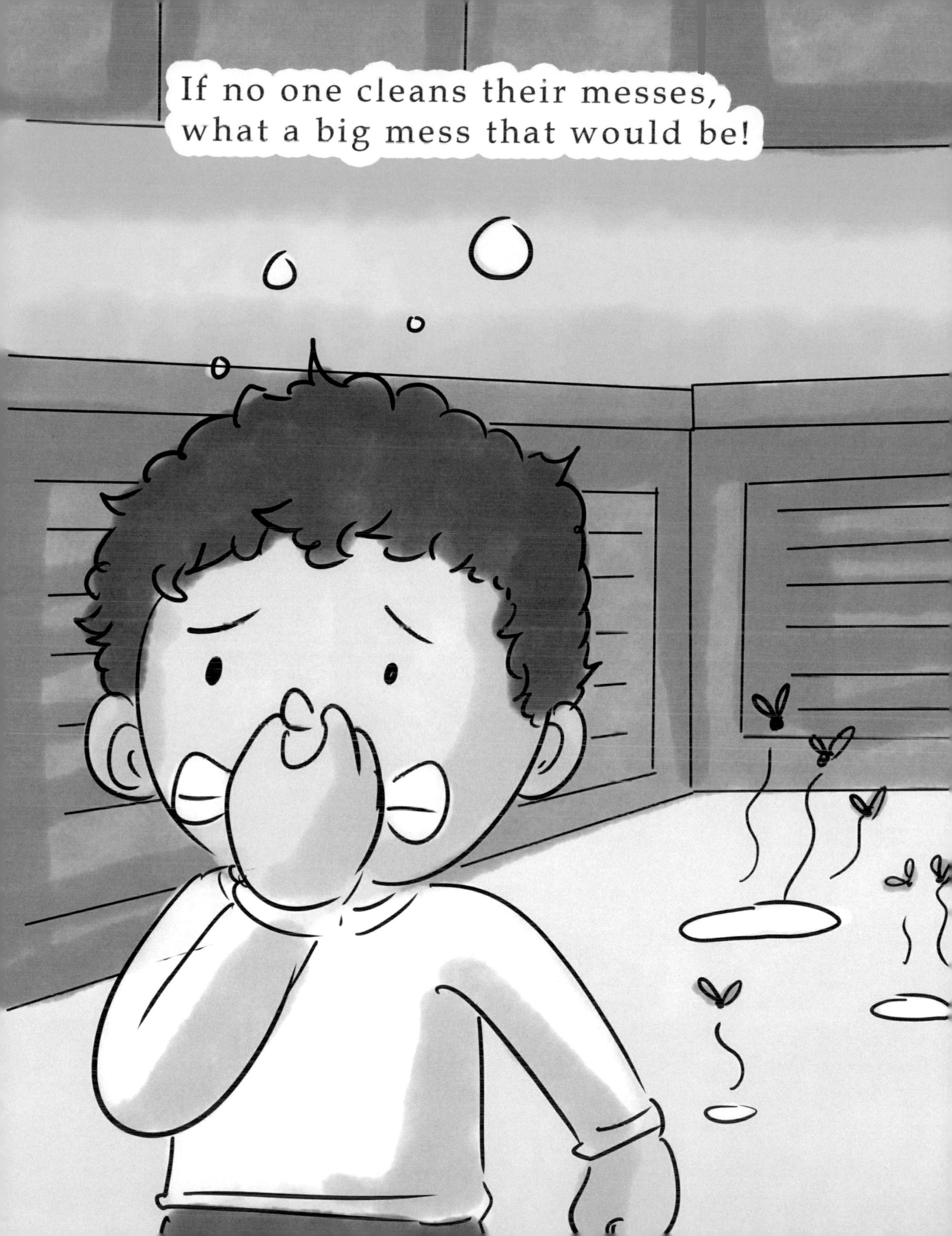

When you cut in line,
you know that it is rude.
Now think about what if everyone
does the same thing to you?

When you take things that you shouldn't,
or don't do what you should,
Then how can people trust you?
Diggory, that's not very good!

Here's a lesson, Diggory Doo, that everyone must learn – *Every choice a person makes will come back in return.*

For instance, think of others first;
I think that you will find,
That you'll get the best results
when you choose to do what's kind.

So be careful of the choices
that you have to make each day,
For when you choose to do what's right,
then good things come your way!

RESPONSIBLE

KIND

HONEST

Just picture for a moment,
if we all choose to agree...
To always make good choices,
what a fine world this would be!

Get your FREE Gift from Diggory Doo at
www.MyDragonBooks.com/gift

Read more about Drew and Diggory Doo!

Visit
www.MyDragonBooks.com
for more!

Made in the USA
Middletown, DE
14 February 2019